ROYAL RESCUES

The Naughty Kitten

Paula Harrison

illustrated by Olivia Chin Mueller

Feiwel and Friends • New York

For Isla Maher, who loves cats

A Feiwel and Friends Book
An imprint of Macmillan Publishing Group, LLC
120 Broadway, New York, NY 10271

Library of Congress Control Number: 2019948761

ISBN 978-1-250-26488-6 (hardcover)
1 3 5 7 9 10 8 6 4 2

ISBN 978-1-250-25923-3 (trade paperback)
3 5 7 9 10 8 6 4 2

ISBN 978-1-250-25924-0 (ebook)

Book design by Nosy Crow
Feiwel and Friends logo designed by Filomena Tuosto

First published in the UK by Nosy Crow as
Princess of Pets: The Naughty Kitten in 2019.
mackids.com

Chapter One

The Animal-Mad Princess

Bea raced across the royal garden with a mouse-shaped kite in her hand. Its pink ears fluttered and its ribbon tail waved in the breeze. Her younger brother, Alfie, ran after her, holding a dinosaur kite over his head.

The round golden towers of Ruby Palace gleamed in the sunshine behind them, and little puffs of white cloud were sailing across the bright blue sky. It was perfect weather for kite flying!

"Wait for us, please, Princess Beatrice," called Mr. Wells, the royal tutor, walking down the path with Natasha, Bea's older sister.

Nine-year-old Bea was the middle child of the three royal children. Their mother had died from a fever when Alfie was tiny, so they lived at Ruby Palace with their father, King George, and all the royal servants. Most mornings were spent in lessons with Mr. Wells in the palace schoolroom, but today they were having a special trip to the Savara Kite Festival.

Bea reached the palace gate and tapped her foot impatiently. Mr. Wells and Natasha were walking so slowly! Jenny, one of the palace maids, was following them with a picnic basket full of goodies for lunch.

Climbing onto the gate, Bea gazed down the hill at the town. Savara was a large cluster of shops and houses, beside a long, sandy beach edged with palm trees. The harbor next to the beach was full of colorful fishing boats.

Everything looked very small from the top of the hill. There were rows of little red rooftops, a green square, which was the park, and streets full of tiny people. Beyond that was the sea, sparkling like diamonds.

Posters about the Savara Kite Festival had been hanging up in the town for weeks. The festival was starting at eleven o'clock, and there would be a prize for the best kite flying and for the most interesting homemade kite.

Bea had built her kite in the shape of a giant mouse, with whiskers made from drinking straws and a brown ribbon tail. The kite looked like Fluff, the mouse she kept under her bed. Bea was animal-mad and loved every creature she met, from squirrels to ladybugs. But every time she begged her dad to let her have a pet, his answer was always the same: *I'm sorry, Beatrice, but the royal palace is no place for a pet.*

So Bea had begun secretly looking after any animal that needed her help. She'd rescued Fluff from a lonely hole behind the piano in the dining room, and now he slept in a cardboard box under her bed. She'd saved Crinkly the spider before the housekeeper could reach him with her broom.

She'd also built a nest in the garden shed for some doves whose tree had blown down in a storm.

Bea loved Fluff and Crinkly, but she still longed for more pets. She wished she had a gorgeous furry rabbit or a beautiful pony with a soft white mane.

Sometimes she talked to Alfie about the animals she rescued, but she never told Natasha. Her sister loved being in charge and never broke royal rules. If she heard about Bea's animals, she might tell Mrs. Stickler. The royal housekeeper hated anything that caused a mess and was sure to banish any creature from the palace immediately.

"Look, Bea!" Alfie pointed to a dragon kite gliding in the distance. The sunlight glinted on its bright red scales and spiky tail.

"They've started the festival!" Bea yanked the gate open. "Mr. Wells, can we meet you at the bottom of the hill?"

"All right," the teacher replied. "But be careful not to slip and . . ."

Bea raced through the gate, missing the rest of her teacher's words. The wind whistled in her ears, and Alfie's feet thudded on the path behind her. They passed street after street until they reached the park, which was full of kites and people.

A gray-haired lady with a clipboard stopped them just inside the park gate. "Hello, I'm Mrs. Brown, and I'm running the festival. Could I have your names, please, and a brief description of your kites?"

"I'm Bea, and this is Fluff the giant mouse," said Bea, holding out her kite.

"I'm Alfie, and this is Mr. Triceratops. Rahhh!" Alfie shook his kite as he roared.

Jenny hurried up behind them with the picnic basket. "Actually, that should be *Princess* Beatrice and *Prince* Alfred," she told Mrs. Brown. "And Princess Natasha will be here in just a moment."

Mrs. Brown peered at Alfie and Bea.

"Your Royal Highnesses! I almost didn't recognize you."

Bea watched eagerly as the dragon kite soared over their heads. "Can we start flying our kites now?"

"Of course you can! Just find an open space so that your kite doesn't get tangled with any others." Mrs. Brown turned to Natasha as she walked primly through the park gate. "Good morning, Princess Natasha. Are you flying a kite, too?"

"No, but I'd love to help with the judging." Natasha's eyes gleamed.

"Oh! Well, I don't see why not," said Mrs. Brown. "Mr. Patel from the bakery is our official judge, but I'm sure he'd love some help."

"I think I'll be really good at it!" said Natasha. "Can I borrow a clipboard so I can make some notes?"

Bea looked for somewhere to fly her kite, but every time she found an empty space, another kite swooped past. At last she found a place at the edge of the park and unwound her kite string. After waiting for a strong gust of wind, she tossed her mouse kite into the air. It hung there for a moment, its whiskers quivering. Then the breeze caught it and it soared into the sky.

Bea let the string out gently and then tugged it to help the kite catch the wind again. The mouse kite was flying!

A seagull glided past, flying toward the harbor. Bea heard shouts and laughter all around her, but she never took her eyes off her kite. It would be amazing if she could make it loop the loop. She had once seen a kite flier do awesome stunts with their kite, and she wanted to try that, too.

She'd decided to be brave and try when a huge gust of wind blew in from the sea. The gust took hold of Bea's kite, tugging it along. Bea hung on to the string, and she was dragged along, too. The kite spiraled around and around like water going down a drain. Then it twisted sideways and blew straight into a tree.

"Bother!" cried Bea, tugging on the string.

The kite was wedged between two branches. Bea pulled again, but nothing happened, so she stopped, afraid she might break the string. The tree had plenty of low branches, so she could just climb up and grab it. But what if Mr. Wells got upset when he saw her scrambling up a tree?

She glanced around. Mr. Wells was

watching the dragon kite with Natasha, who was busy scribbling notes on her clipboard. Bea climbed the tree swiftly and took hold of the kite. When it still wouldn't move, she clambered a little higher, hoping to free the kite without tearing the cloth. A gust of wind rocked the tree, and Bea held on tight. Branches creaked, and the leaves over her head rustled.

The gust of wind faded, but the leaves above her kept on rustling. Bea looked up just as a little furry face with big green eyes popped out from between the branches. It was a tiny kitten with beautiful stripy orange fur. The kitten meowed sadly, its gaze fixed on Bea.

"Oh, hello, kitten! What are you doing up here?" asked Bea in surprise. "Are you stuck?"

The kitten gave a tiny, shaky meow. Another blast of wind hit the tree, and the branches swung wildly. The kitten crouched low, staring around with wide eyes. Its tiny claws gripped tightly to a branch.

A cold prickle ran down Bea's back. She had to get the little cat to safety! The wind was growing stronger, and the kitten was in terrible danger.

Chapter Two

Pets and Picnics

The kitten's big green eyes grew even wider as Bea edged along the branch. She held out her hand, letting the kitten sniff it. "Don't worry!" she said softly. "I'll get you down from there."

The kitten meowed and rubbed its head against her hand. Bea's heart melted. This was the most adorable cat ever!

"Princess Beatrice, please come down!" Mr. Wells called from the bottom of the tree. "I really don't think climbing up there was a good idea."

Bea held on tight as another gust of wind swept by. "Just a minute!" she yelled down. "There's a little kitten—I can't just leave it here."

"Princess Beatrice, please be careful!" Jenny squeaked.

"It's all right. I'll be down in a second." Bea climbed to a higher branch. She had to grab the little animal without letting go of the tree. If the kitten panicked and tried to climb out of reach, this could get very tricky indeed.

"It's okay, little kitty. Everything will be fine." She reached out and slipped her hand under the kitten's fluffy belly, scooping it up. Holding the creature close, she climbed down the tree using one hand.

A round of applause broke out as she

reached the ground. Turning around, she found a crowd of people watching.

"Honestly, Princess Beatrice!" Mr. Wells had gone pale. "What would your father, King George, say if he was here? I'm sure you do these sorts of things to frighten me."

"And to show off," said Natasha.

Bea ignored her sister. "Sorry, Mr. Wells! I really didn't mean to scare you. Does anyone know who this kitten belongs to?"

No one replied, and a few people shook their heads. Bea frowned. The kitten didn't have a collar, but she was sure it had to belong to somebody.

"Come and have some lunch, Princess Beatrice," said Jenny. "I've set out the picnic."

"And you can put the cat down now,"

added Natasha. "Oh, is that your kite stuck in the tree?"

But Bea didn't want to put the kitten down, and she didn't mind so much about her kite anymore. After all, kittens were a lot more important than kites. She held the little orange cat close to her chest as she sank onto the picnic blanket.

"Did you see Mr. Triceratops do that loop the loop?" Alfie ran up with the dinosaur kite under his arm. "Hey, where did you get that kitten?"

"I rescued it from that tree over there," Bea told him.

"It's a very lucky kitten, and you're very lucky not to have fallen out of the tree." Jenny passed around cups of lemonade. "I didn't know you were so good at climbing."

Bea smiled to herself. She climbed trees

in the palace garden all the time when the grown-ups weren't looking. Alfie started helping himself to the picnic. There were sandwiches, jars of raspberry jelly, and a plate of chocolate muffins.

The kitten wriggled, trying to climb over Bea's shoulder. Bea stroked its soft orange fur until it settled down in her lap. The kitten purred so loudly that Bea could feel it from its head right down to its lovely stripy tail.

"We'll return to the palace right after the picnic," said Mr. Wells. "I shall be glad when we're back there safe and sound."

"But Mrs. Brown said I could announce the prize winners with Mr. Patel," cried Natasha.

"And I have to find out who this kitten

belongs to." Bea finished her sandwich and jumped to her feet. She walked around the park, asking everyone if they knew who owned the kitten, but no one could help.

More flying displays began. A majestic eagle kite with enormous wings soared upward. It glided across the sky, performing three somersaults in a row. The crowd clapped eagerly. A teddy-bear kite flew into the air next, followed by a plane kite with stripy blue-and-yellow wings.

Finally, the dragon kite took to the

air again. Its red scales glinted with each twist and turn, and its spiky tail flicked in the wind. The crowd gasped as it dived right over their heads. Everyone applauded the kite flier—a gray-haired lady in a green sweater.

Mr. Patel stepped forward and raised his hand for quiet. "Thank you, everyone! I'm sure you'll agree this has been a really exciting day. I'm pleased that Princess Natasha, who's helped a great deal with the judging, will now present the prizes."

Natasha beamed as she stepped forward, holding the medals. "The first prize for kite acrobatics goes to . . ." She paused dramatically. "The flier of the dragon kite!"

Bea nodded as everyone clapped. The dragon kite had been amazing. The kitten wriggled in her arms but calmed down as Bea stroked him softly under the chin.

"Oh, Princess Beatrice!" Mrs. Brown hurried past. "I see you're still carrying that kitten around."

"No one seems to know where he came from," Bea explained.

"Well, he's much too small to find his own way home," said Mrs. Brown. "I think Mr. Patel has an empty shed at the back of his bakery. Perhaps we can keep the little cat in there until we find his owner. I'll ask him now!"

Bea stared after her in dismay. She knew Mrs. Brown was only trying to help, but she didn't think the kitten should be kept in a cold shed for the night. It didn't sound very comfortable at all! What if the poor thing got lonely or scared? She was determined that the kitten should be cared for properly.

"Hey, Bea!" Alfie ran up to her. "Look—I got your kite out of the tree."

"Thanks, Alfie," said Bea.

Alfie spun the two kites over his head. "Bother! Mr. Wells is waving at us. I think he wants to leave."

Bea bit her lip. Mrs. Brown might come back at any moment to take the kitten to Mr. Patel's shed. She really couldn't let the little animal be taken away! But her dad would never let her keep a cat at Ruby Palace. He would say what he always said: *Beatrice, the royal palace is no place for a pet.*

Alfie opened the picnic basket and peered in. "Rats! There's nothing left. Natasha must have eaten that last muffin."

Bea stared at the picnic basket. If she took the kitten back home, it would only be for a short time . . . just until she found the animal's real owner. Her heart beat faster. "You need lots of love and attention, don't you?" she whispered into the kitten's ear. "Don't worry. I'll look after you!"

She glanced at Jenny, who'd turned away to shake the crumbs off the picnic blanket. None of the grown-ups were looking! Bea quickly bent down and popped the kitten inside the picnic basket. Then she shut the lid firmly.

Jenny folded up the blanket and glanced at Bea. "I'm glad you gave that kitten back, Princess Bea. I think we're ready to go." She reached for the handle of the basket.

"It's all right—I'll carry it." Bea picked up the basket.

Alfie giggled and stared at the basket. “I can help! Let me hold it.”

“You’re carrying the kites.” Bea shot her brother a look, warning him not to give anything away.

The kitten scratched the inside of the basket and then began to meow. Natasha looked around suspiciously, so Bea started humming to cover the sound. She let the others walk ahead as they climbed the hill to the palace.

“Shall I take the picnic basket to the kitchen, Princess Beatrice?” asked Jenny as they reached the palace steps.

“I guess so.” Bea let Jenny take the basket, annoyed that she couldn’t think of a reason to say no. “But I’ll come with you. I . . . um . . . just need a glass of water.”

“Please come to the schoolroom once

you've had a drink, Princess Beatrice," said Mr. Wells. "We must complete our history lesson."

Bea followed Jenny to the kitchen. She desperately hoped the kitten didn't start meowing again. How was she going to get the little cat out of the basket without anyone seeing?

Chapter Three

Feeding a Tiger

Bea's heart sank as she followed Jenny into the palace kitchen. Mrs. Stickler, the royal housekeeper, was talking to the palace chef. Bea was certain neither of them would be happy to see the kitten. Mrs. Stickler didn't like animals, and Chef Darou hated anything messing up his kitchen.

"I want you to make sure tonight's dinner has lots of vegetables." The housekeeper brushed a speck of dust off her perfectly neat blouse. Her sharp eyes darted around the kitchen.

"King George wants everything to be healthy and nutritious. Perhaps the meal could begin with vegetable soup, followed by a stir-fry with rice and beans."

"Rice and beans!" The chef paced up and down, waving his thin arms dramatically. A tall white cook's hat wobbled on his head.

"I've ordered some lovely pieces of salmon from the fishmonger. What am I supposed to do with those now?"

"I don't know! I suppose you'll have to put them in the freezer." Mrs. Stickler passed Bea on the way to the door. "Do you need something, Princess Beatrice? Princes and princesses aren't supposed to come into the kitchen, you know."

There was the sound of an engine outside and brakes squeaking.

Chef Darou raised his hands in mock despair. "Here's the fish van now. Another wonderful menu turns to dust!"

Mrs. Stickler ignored him, her gaze fixed on Bea. "Well, Princess Beatrice? What are you here for?"

"I'm just getting a drink," explained Bea.

"I'll get that for you." Jenny set down

the picnic basket and took a glass from the cupboard.

Mrs. Stickler left the room, and Chef Darou marched outside to the fish van, still muttering to himself. Bea grabbed a tea towel and edged toward the basket. Checking that Jenny wasn't watching, she opened the lid and scooped up the kitten before he could run away. The little cat gave an indignant meow and scrabbled at Bea's arm with his tiny paws. Bea quickly wrapped the kitten in the tea towel till only a tiny pair of eyes and ears stuck out of the top.

"Did you hear that?" Jenny swung around. "It sounded like an animal."

"Really?" Bea hid the tea towel. "I don't think I heard anything."

Jenny handed her the glass of water and then hurried outside to help Chef Darou. She returned a moment later and set a box of fish on the table. There were fresh haddock, smoked mackerel, peeled shrimp, and long strips of pink salmon. The smell of fish filled the room. The kitten wriggled wildly, and Bea realized how hungry he must be.

Suddenly, she noticed Jenny watching her. She must have been standing there, just staring at the fish! Worried that the kitten might meow again, Bea backed away. "Thanks, Jenny!" She dashed out the door and ran right upstairs to her bedroom.

Shutting her door, she took the kitten out of the tea towel and set him down on the bed. "There you are—you're safe at last!"

The little cat prowled across her pillow. Then he lost his balance and tumbled down the other side. Bea rescued him before he got stuck in the gap between the bed and the wall. The kitten meowed and gazed around in surprise.

There was a rustling from Fluff's box, and Bea suddenly realized that having the kitten around could be dangerous for the mouse. She took Fluff's house—a tattered cardboard box—from under the bed and hurried down the corridor to Alfie's room.

Alfie was setting up a battle of plastic dinosaurs on his bed.

"Aren't you supposed to be in the schoolroom?" said Bea.

"Yeah, but so are you!" Alfie added a T-Rex to the battle. "Where's the kitten?"

"I'm keeping him in my room for now," Bea explained. "That's why I need you to have Fluff. Please look after him carefully!"

Alfie jumped up and took the cardboard box. Fluff poked his little pink nose out from under the lid, his whiskers quivering. "Cool! Can I feed him anything?"

"There's some cereal in there already, and sometimes he likes a bit of fruit, especially banana." Bea rubbed her forehead. She needed to get the kitten some food, too. "And can you cover for me with Mr. Wells? I need to find the kitten something to eat."

"In a minute!" Alfie went back to his dinosaurs.

Bea frowned as she ran downstairs. She wanted to pick something out of the fishmonger's box, but which fish would the kitten like best, and how much could she take without Chef Darou noticing?

The kitchen was empty, but Bea knew the chef could be back at any moment. Searching around, she discovered the fish at the back of the freezer. She gazed at the rows of haddock and shrimp, and shivered as the icy air drifted over her. She took out the pink salmon and wrapped two long strips in a tea towel. Then she gathered two bowls from the cupboard and dashed back to her room.

The little cat was still exploring her

bed, frisking up and down and sniffing the pillow.

"I'm afraid it's been in the freezer," Bea told the cat as she laid the fish in one of the bowls and put it on the window seat. "But it wasn't in there for long, and maybe the sun will warm it."

The kitten caught the scent of the fish. Meowing excitedly, he tried to jump off the bed, but he slipped and had to cling to the edge with his paws.

"Careful, silly!" Bea lifted him down and placed him on the floor. Then she filled the second bowl with water.

The kitten jumped onto the window seat and began to lick the salmon. His beautiful orange fur gleamed in the sunshine.

Bea sat down beside him. "I think I'll call you Tiger. It goes with your lovely stripy fur, and you climbed up that tree just like a real tiger!" She stroked Tiger's soft coat, and the kitten flicked his tail gently.

At last Bea reluctantly got to her feet. She really wanted to stay and play with Tiger, but she was supposed to be in the schoolroom. What if Mr. Wells got suspicious and came looking for her? "I'll be back soon," she promised the kitten.

When Bea came back after her lessons, Tiger had disappeared. She looked under the bed and behind the wardrobe, but there was no sign of the kitten. She stared around the room, her forehead creasing. The door had been shut, so surely Tiger couldn't have escaped.

"Tiger!" she called softly. "Where are you?"

There was no answering meow.

Bea opened her chest of drawers just in case the kitten had clambered inside somehow. "Tiger? Where did you go?"

She listened carefully, and her heart thumped in the silence. What if someone had come in and seen the kitten? If it was Mrs. Stickler, she would have taken Tiger away at once.

There was a sudden scratching noise at the top of the wardrobe. Bea's heart skipped when Tiger's furry face peeped

over the edge. The kitten gave a tiny, pitiful meow.

"How did you get up there?" cried Bea, lifting Tiger off. "You really shouldn't climb on things if you can't get yourself down again."

Tiger waved his tail happily. Skipping over to his water bowl, he lapped up the water with his little pink tongue. Then he scampered over to the chair and scratched the chair legs with his little claws.

"Hey, don't do that!" Bea stared at the scratch marks. Mrs. Stickler was bound to notice them. What did the scratching mean? Was the kitten bored? Did he need some toys to play with?

Tiger began pouncing on the curtains and diving under them with an excited squeak that made Bea smile. Then the kitten began climbing up one of the curtains, digging his claws into the material.

Bea lifted him down, laughing. "I didn't know kittens liked to climb so much." She suddenly wondered if she ought to know more about kittens. It would help her look after Tiger better. There might be something about caring for cats in the palace library.

Bea decided that Tiger might get stuck somewhere if he was left alone again, so she popped the kitten into a cloth bag. Tiger gave a protesting meow before settling down inside the bag and closing his eyes. Bea checked that the corridor was empty before slipping out of her room with the tiny kitten at her side.

Chapter Four

Big Cats and Little Cats

Bea crept down the palace stairs with the kitten curled up inside her bag. She slipped through the door to the library. Towering bookcases stood in rows, and the arched windows let in beams of sunlight that made a pattern across the wooden floor.

"Bea!" Alfie came running in. "What are you doing?"

"Looking for a book about cats. Shh!

The kitten's asleep." Bea let him peep into the bag. "I'm calling him Tiger because of his stripy fur."

"Tiger's a silly name," said Alfie.

"I think it suits him. Anyway, I'm looking for information to help me take care of him properly." Bea searched the shelves and found the books on animals and wildlife.

"Look at this one!" Alfie waved a book with a leopard on the front. "It's called *Big Cats and Little Cats*."

"That's great!" Bea took it and leafed through the pages. The book had chapters on lions, leopards, and tigers, *and* a chapter on pet cats. "It says here that cats often behave the same way that lions and tigers do. They love chasing things—especially wool or string—and they love sleeping in warm, cozy places."

"So Tiger really is like a tiger!" Alfie grinned.

Bea turned a page. "It says here that cats often scratch things, and to stop them from damaging the furniture, you can make them a scratching post."

Alfie yawned. "Sounds tricky!"

Bea closed the book. "First I have to find out who Tiger's owner is. Someone in Savara must know who he belongs to. Hey—we should make some lost-kitten posters that we can put up around town!"

"I'm too busy to make posters. See you later!" Alfie ran off.

Bea hurried upstairs to the empty schoolroom. Tiger had woken up, so she lifted the kitten out of the bag and settled down to draw the posters. Tiger prowled up and down the room, sniffing the crayons.

Lost and Found, Bea wrote at the top of the first one. *Have you lost a kitten? He was found in the park and has stripy*

orange fur. Then she drew a picture of Tiger underneath. Finally she wrote, *If this is your cat, come to Ruby Palace to collect him.* Then she drew four more posters and colored them all in, making sure she got the color of Tiger's fur exactly right.

By the time she'd finished, Tiger was playing a game with the crayons. He would pounce on them and roll them along the floor with little swipes of his paws. Bea remembered what the book had said about cats and string. She found a ball of string in Mr. Wells's desk and rolled it along the ground for Tiger to play with.

Next she decided to make a scratching post. She found a roll of wrapping paper and some material in the odds-and-ends box in the schoolroom cupboard.

She twisted the material around the wrapping paper before gluing the tube to a flat piece of cardboard so that it stood up straight.

"There—do you like it, Tiger?" she said, wiping glue off her fingers.

The kitten bounced up to the newly made post and scratched it right away.

"Good boy!" Bea picked up Tiger and hugged him. "Are you hungry yet? I bet you'd like some more fish."

The door creaked open, and King George stood in the doorway. "Beatrice, I just wanted to tell you— Good gracious! What is that animal doing here?"

Bea stared at her dad in horror. Tiger broke free of her arms and jumped to the floor, pouncing on a crayon that had rolled under a table. The king's frown deepened.

"I can explain!" said Bea. "I found this little kitten at the kite festival this morning, but no one knew who he belonged to. I'm going to put these up to find his owner." She showed her dad one of her posters.

The king sighed. "I understand that you want to help the creature, but you know I don't allow animals in the palace. They are simply not appropriate for a royal residence."

"Please, Dad! Tiger's such a lovely kitten. He won't be any trouble, I promise," begged Bea.

The king studied Tiger, who was pulling pieces off the new scratching post with his claws. "I can't change my rules for one animal, Beatrice. Didn't the adults at the kite festival offer to take charge of him?"

Bea hesitated. "Yes, Mrs. Brown wanted to ask Mr. Patel if the kitten could sleep in his shed, but—"

"That would have been a much better plan!" The king shook his head. "Honestly, Beatrice, I really don't understand where you get these ridiculous ideas from."

Bea flushed. She wished her dad could see how much Tiger needed looking after.

"Oh, I almost forgot." King George turned to go, before stopping in the doorway. "I'm about to leave for Lania. I'm going there for the opening ceremony of the new city gardens, and I won't be back till tomorrow. I expect the cat to be gone by the time I return."

Bea's heart sank. What if she hadn't

found the kitten's owner by tomorrow? Then Tiger would have to stay in Mr. Patel's cold, lonely shed.

"Also, don't go into my royal study," the king added. "I've left my crowns out, ready to be polished, and I don't want anyone except the maid to touch them."

"Yes, Dad." Tiger was creeping toward the door, so Bea gathered him up quickly. She hugged the kitten tight as her dad's footsteps faded on the stairs. One day wasn't very much time to find Tiger's owner, but she knew her dad wouldn't change his mind.

Bea stroked Tiger between his ears, and the kitten began to purr. "You just need a good home, don't you? Don't worry—I'll find out where you came

from, and everything will be all right."
With the kitten under one arm, she grabbed her Lost and Found posters and hurried out of the schoolroom.

Chapter Five

Lost and Found

Bea sneaked out of the palace with Alfie, who'd decided that going into town without Mr. Wells would be a great adventure. Bea had reluctantly left Tiger in her bedroom. The little kitten just wanted to play, and Bea worried that if he was taken outside, he might scamper off and get lost somewhere.

Bea took the posters, and Alfie carried a large roll of sticky tape. They stuck one poster on a lamppost on the main street in town, one by the harbor, and one in the park. Then Bea went into the bakery and asked Mr. Patel if she could put one up in the window.

"Of course you can, Princess Beatrice," said Mr. Patel. "I wondered where the little kitten had gone. Mrs. Brown came to ask if I would look after him, but I'm sure you're doing a much better job."

Bea blushed. "I hope you don't mind that I took him with me?"

"Not at all!" cried Mr. Patel. "Would you like to take this cat food that I bought? I picked it up from the corner shop just in case."

"Yes, please!" Bea took the packets of cat food. "Thanks for your help."

Mr. Patel smiled. "Good luck with everything, Princess Beatrice."

Alfie and Bea set off down the main street. "Tiger's owner is sure to see one of the posters," said Bea. "I just hope they see it in time." Her stomach tightened. Her dad would be back tomorrow, and he would expect the kitten to be gone from the palace.

"Hold on, there's one left." Alfie pointed at the last poster. "Where should we put it?"

"We could ask the Makalis if we can put it up in the Sleepy Gull Café." Bea shaded her eyes to look at the pretty wooden café sitting on the cliff top behind the beach. "We'd better hurry, though. If we don't get back in time for dinner, Mrs. Stickler is sure to ask lots of tricky questions about where we've been."

Alfie and Bea climbed the steep cliff path. Patches of sea thrift bloomed

beside the footpath like little pink lollipops. The waves made a gentle *shhh* as they lapped against the beach, and seagulls cried as they swooped overhead. At the top, the path led to the café, which had pots of basil and coriander growing beside the door.

The Sleepy Gull Café was one of Bea's

favorite places because her best friend, Keira, lived there. She and Bea had been friends for years, and Keira loved visiting Ruby Palace almost as much as Bea loved coming to the café. Keira's parents, Mr. and Mrs. Makali, cooked lots of dishes. The spicy spring rolls and crumbly chocolate brownies were among Bea's favorites.

Bea made her way into the café, breathing in the delicious cooking smells.

"Bea!" Keira ran out from behind the counter. She had smiling brown eyes, and her long hair was pulled into a ponytail. "Dad's been making a fresh batch of tacos. Would you and Alfie like one?"

"They smell amazing! But we actually came to ask you a favor. Please, could we put a poster up on your wall?" Bea explained about rescuing Tiger from the tree. "I hope Tiger's owner will see one of the posters. No one at the kite festival knew where he came from."

Keira's eyes widened. "Poor little kitten! I'll ask Mom and Dad about the poster." She disappeared into the kitchen.

Bea couldn't hear their conversation over the sounds of chopping and sizzling. Keira came out a moment later with her mom.

"Of course you can put up your poster, Princess Bea," said Mrs. Makali, straightening her flowery apron. "Then you and Prince Alfie must have some pineapple milkshake. It's the latest new flavor I'm trying out."

Bea stuck the poster on the café wall, and she, Keira, and Alfie drank the delicious pineapple milkshake. Then Bea said goodbye to her friend, and she and Alfie hurried along the cliff path toward the palace. The sun was already sinking in the sky, and they didn't dare be late for dinner.

They took a shortcut and climbed into the palace garden, scrambling down a plum tree that grew right beside the wall.

Bea jumped down first, and as she landed, she spotted someone in a gray jacket moving among the trees. "Hello, is that you, Mrs. Cherry?" she called, expecting it to be the palace gardener.

Leaves rustled and the figure moved out of sight.

"That was strange," said Bea. "Maybe it was one of the grooms from the stables."

"What was strange?" Alfie twisted around as he jumped from the tree.

He lost his balance and landed with a bump. "Ouch! It's all right—I'm okay."

Bea noticed a scrape on his leg as she pulled him up. "You've cut your knee. Let's go inside and get you a Band-Aid."

They'd just reached the palace steps when Mrs. Stickler came rushing out of the front entrance. She looked them over with a sharp frown. "Princess Beatrice, before the king left he told me all about the stray cat you brought back here. I'm very pleased to see you've followed his orders and gotten rid of the creature."

Bea went red. Mrs. Stickler clearly didn't know that Tiger was still inside Bea's room. "The thing is—" she began, but the housekeeper cut her off.

"There's nothing worse than having to clear up a lot of mess left by an animal," Mrs. Stickler said sternly.

Bea had been just about to tell the housekeeper that Tiger was still upstairs, but she stopped herself. Mrs. Stickler disliked animals so much that she might decide to throw the kitten out of the palace immediately.

"Bea, my knee's starting to hurt. Can you find me a Band-Aid?" Alfie winced as he limped toward the stairs.

"Sorry, Mrs. Stickler. I've got to go." Bea rushed after her brother and helped him along the corridor.

Maybe the Lost and Found posters would do the trick and Tiger's owner would come knocking on the palace door. But if they didn't, Bea was determined to keep the kitten safely hidden until tomorrow.

Chapter Six

The Great Curtain Climb

Tiger was waiting there as soon as Bea opened her bedroom door. The kitten fixed his green eyes on Bea and gave a long, reproachful meow. Then he scratched at the homemade scratching post with his little claws.

"What's wrong, Tiger?" Alfie sank into a chair and examined his cut knee.

"His food bowl is empty. He must have finished the last bit of salmon while we were out." Bea rummaged in the drawers, found a box of Band-Aids, and handed one to Alfie. "Here you go."

"Thanks." Alfie stuck the Band-Aid on his knee and limped to the door.

Bea shut the door behind Alfie, careful not to let Tiger out. Then she turned to the little kitten and rustled the shopping bag with the cat food inside. "Hey, Tiger! Guess what I've got in here."

Tiger scampered across the room, paying no attention to Bea. He began climbing the curtains, gripping onto them with his sharp claws. He scrambled onto the curtain rod at the top and balanced there with a triumphant meow.

"You are silly!" cried Bea. "You won't be able to get down from there by yourself."

Tiger meowed again and disappeared

behind the curtain ruffles at the end of the rod.

There was a knock at the door. Bea quickly hid the shopping bag under her pillow. "Who is it?"

"It's me!" said Natasha. "Mrs. Stickler wanted me to tell you dinner's at five thirty."

"Okay, I won't be long," Bea called back.

"Who are you talking to in there?" said Natasha.

"No one! I'll come downstairs in a minute." Bea looked around in a panic. If Natasha burst in, like she sometimes did, there would be no time to get Tiger down from the curtain rod. Swiftly, she hid the homemade scratching post under her bed.

The door swung open, and Natasha looked around the room suspiciously. "It really sounded like you were speaking to someone."

"I was just talking to myself." Bea shrugged.

Natasha folded her arms. "Mrs. Stickler told me that you brought that kitten home from the kite festival. I knew you were up to something this morning."

Bea glanced at the curtain rod, her heart racing. Thankfully, Tiger was still hidden behind the ruffles. "I should get changed for dinner . . ."

"Don't be upset that Dad made you take the kitten back," Natasha went on. "The rule is there can't be any pets in the palace. If there were animals running around everywhere, they'd get in the way every time we had important visitors."

Bea spotted the curtain ruffles twitching. Tiger might appear at any moment, and then her sister would tell Mrs. Stickler that the kitten was still here. Bea steered Natasha away and started closing the door. "Well, thanks for telling me about dinner . . ."

"Hey, Bea!" Alfie came down the corridor. "Did Tiger like the cat food?"

Natasha frowned deeply. "Who's Tiger? What have you done, Bea?"

Bea sighed. She might have known Alfie would give the game away. "Tiger's the kitten's name. He's still here because I haven't found his owner yet."

Tiger's furry face popped out from behind the curtain ruffles, and his tail swayed like a little branch in the wind. He meowed sadly and gazed at Bea.

Climbing onto a chair, Bea reached

out for the kitten. "It's all right! Just hold still." She lifted Tiger down from the rod and cuddled him gently.

"Oh, Bea! Mrs. Stickler will be so mad when she finds out," cried Natasha. "She thinks

you've already given the kitten away like you were supposed to."

"But Dad only said he should be gone by tomorrow . . . and look how small he is!" Bea brought the kitten closer to her sister. "I couldn't just leave him alone somewhere. He needs to be looked after properly."

Tiger snuggled in Bea's arms and purred. Then he began licking his paws with his little pink tongue.

"Please don't tell Mrs. Stickler," begged Bea. "It's only for one day, and I promise he won't cause any trouble."

Natasha softened. "He's really cute! I've never seen a cat with such stripy orange fur before."

"That's why he's called Tiger," said Alfie.

"Can I hold him, too?" Natasha made a grab for the kitten, and Tiger stiffened and gave a sharp yowl.

"Sorry!" Bea made a face. "Maybe Tiger's not used to lots of different people yet."

Alfie laughed. "Ha-ha! Cats don't like you!"

Natasha's smile vanished. "He's not a very nice cat, is he? I don't think you should be breaking royal rules like this, Bea. If that animal makes a lot of mess, don't expect me to cover for you!"

Bea's heart sank as Natasha marched off. "You shouldn't have said that cats don't like her," she told Alfie.

"I was only joking." Alfie looked around. "So where's the new cat food?"

Bea set Tiger down on the carpet and pulled the shopping bag from underneath her pillow. "This is chicken flavor. I hope he likes it."

"Can I do it?" Alfie pulled a packet open and poured some food into Tiger's bowl. "There you go, kitty. Dinnertime!"

Tiger took no notice. He pounced on a scrap of paper lying on the carpet as if it were a mouse. Then he hurtled around the room, diving under Alfie's legs and making him laugh. Bea tried to catch him, but the kitten slipped through her fingers and ran off down the corridor.

"Tiger, wait!" Bea raced after the kitten, her heart pounding. What if Tiger got lost? What if Natasha saw the cat running around everywhere and told Mrs. Stickler?

She had to catch Tiger before the kitten turned Ruby Palace upside down!

Chapter Seven

A Kitten on the Loose

Bea stared around the passageway, desperately wondering where Tiger had gone. Then she spotted a flash of orange fur behind a bookcase. The kitten scampered out of hiding and scratched an expensive-looking chair. Bea winced. Mrs. Stickler was bound to notice those scratch marks!

Next Tiger leapt onto a side table and peered into a gold-painted vase.

Bea crept up to the kitten, planning to catch him while he wasn't looking. But as soon as she got close, Tiger sprang off the table and darted toward the stairs.

Alfie, whose knee seemed much better, ran after Bea. "Let me help!" he yelled. "I'll catch him!"

Bea didn't wait for him. Her stomach was churning. What if Tiger ran outside? The palace gardens were so big he was sure to get lost somewhere.

Tiger raced down the stairs, and Bea and Alfie chased after him. Alfie tried to overtake his sister by leaping down the last two steps. He lost his balance and banged his injured knee on the floor. "Ouch!" he cried, clutching his leg.

Tiger jumped in surprise and ran behind a shoe rack. Then he peeked over the top of the king's Wellington boots, his whiskers trembling.

"Prince Alfred, what on earth is the matter?" Mrs. Stickler came rushing out of the dining room. "For a moment I thought something terrible had happened."

"Sorry!" Alfie rubbed his knee. "I just banged my leg."

"Then perhaps you should try coming downstairs a little more carefully," said the housekeeper sharply. "I hope you weren't chasing him, Princess Beatrice."

"No, I wasn't. I promise!" Bea edged in front of the shoe rack to hide the kitten from view. She really hoped Tiger didn't move until Mrs. Stickler went away.

"Well, I hope you aren't coming to dinner dressed in those dusty clothes," said the housekeeper. "Dinner's in twenty minutes, so there's plenty of time to change."

Bea tried to think of an excuse for staying downstairs. "I'm just looking for my sweater. I think I left it somewhere." She pretended to look around.

There was a scraping noise from the shoe rack behind her, and a Wellington boot slowly toppled to the floor.

Luckily, Mrs. Stickler was brushing dust off a picture frame and didn't notice the fallen boot. She inspected the gray fluff on her finger and tutted. "Nancy!" she called. "You didn't dust properly over here."

Nancy scurried out of the king's study with a cleaning cloth. Through the doorway, Bea saw a row of gold and silver crowns laid out on the desk. Each one sparkled with rubies, emeralds, and diamonds.

"Sorry, Mrs. Stickler," said Nancy. "I was just polishing the king's crowns. I'll clean the picture frames now." She swept the cloth along each frame.

Bea caught a flash of something gray outside the study window, but

she was worrying about Tiger too much to wonder what it was. "Try to catch the kitten!" she muttered to Alfie. "I'll keep Mrs. Stickler busy."

Alfie peered at the shoe rack. "I think Tiger's gone," he whispered back. "I can't see him anywhere."

Bea's heart thudded. Nudging Alfie aside, she crouched down to look under the shoe rack. Tiger had been there just a second ago! Surely he couldn't have disappeared that fast.

"Princess Beatrice, what on earth are you doing?" snapped the housekeeper.

"Um . . . I just wondered if my sweater was down here," said Bea.

"I don't understand how the two of you lose things so easily." Mrs. Stickler turned back to the maid. "Have you finished now, Nancy?"

Bea looked around frantically. Then she spotted the boot that had fallen off the rack. It was twitching and wobbling. Then it jumped forward, as if there was a frog inside it. Bea's heart leapt. Tiger must have burrowed his way inside the boot!

Alfie giggled, and Bea tried to shush him.

"There's nothing funny about dusting, Prince Alfred!" Mrs. Stickler frowned. "Please let Nancy concentrate on what she's doing. It's very important that the palace is absolutely spotless at all times."

"Yes, Mrs. Stickler." Alfie sidled toward the boot with the kitten inside, but Mrs. Stickler reached for it first.

"Here, you can put this back where it belongs." She bent down to pick up the boot just as a little orange paw poked out of the top.

Bea panicked. "DUST!" she shrieked, pointing to a cabinet filled with china plates. "Look, there's dust right there!"

Mrs. Stickler turned around to look at the cabinet. The boot performed a funny one-footed jig behind her. Nancy saw it moving and stared, round-eyed.

"Princess Be-a-trice." The housekeeper pronounced Bea's name very slowly. "If you're overexcited, I suggest you go and lie down before dinner."

"Yes, Mrs. Stickler—sorry!" Bea edged past her and grabbed the boot, holding

it tightly as she hurried back upstairs. Luckily, Mrs. Stickler was too busy staring at the imaginary dust on the cabinet to watch her closely.

Bea didn't stop running until she reached her bedroom. Then she sank onto the bed and tried to get her breath back. Tiger popped his head out of the boot, and his little nose twitched.

"Are you going to spend five minutes without getting into trouble?" Bea smiled as she lifted the kitten out of the boot and gave him a cuddle. Then she set Tiger down beside his food bowl and went to the window.

Daylight was fading outside. A man in a gray jacket was walking across the palace drive. Bea's heart lifted for a moment as she wondered whether he'd seen her Lost and Found posters.

Maybe he had some information about who Tiger belonged to. But the man turned away from the palace steps and disappeared behind a line of trees.

Bea didn't eat much dinner, because she wanted to get back to Tiger as quickly as she could. The kitten seemed happy, though, and spent the evening exploring Bea's bedroom. His favorite pastime was still climbing the curtains, but he also liked clambering up the bookcase and onto the wardrobe. He would shake his whiskers happily every time he reached the top before meowing sadly because he didn't dare jump down again. Each time, Bea laughed and climbed up to rescue him.

Bea made Tiger a kitten bed using an empty cardboard box from the pantry with a blanket stuffed inside. At last

Tiger grew tired and snuggled down on the soft blanket. Bea opened the window a little to let in the cool breeze. Lying down in bed, she watched the moon rise above the palace garden.

Tiger was such a lovely pet. Bea wished with all her heart that somewhere out there was a good home for the little kitten.

Chapter Eight

A Leap in the Dark

Bea woke up in the middle of the night to find the moon shining through her bedroom window. She peered at Tiger's little cat bed, but she couldn't see the kitten.

Bea switched on her lamp. Tiger's bed really was empty.

"Tiger, where are you?" Bea checked the curtains first, but Tiger wasn't there, and he wasn't hiding under the bed, either.

Bea's heart sank when she noticed the door was ajar. She was sure she'd closed it properly last night, but maybe the breeze from the window had blown it open. She pulled on her slippers, grabbed a flashlight, and slipped out of her room.

Every step she took seemed to echo in the silent corridor. The flashlight beam flickered across the palace paintings and the side table with the priceless vase. Bea shone the beam into every corner, hoping to see a flash of stripy fur. She stopped every few steps to listen for meowing or the sound of Tiger padding along the carpet.

She reached the stairs without seeing any sign of the kitten. Shining the flashlight down the steps, she caught her breath. Everything looked so strange in the dark. The flashlight beam caught on the gold picture frames and the silver stair rail, making them gleam like treasure.

A snapping sound made Bea jump.

That didn't sound like Tiger . . . unless he'd knocked something over. Bea hurried down the steps, whispering, "Tiger, is that you?"

She stopped at the bottom and shone the flashlight around again. She wasn't sure which way the noise had come from. She was about to whisper Tiger's name again when she noticed a thin sliver of light along the bottom of the door to her dad's study. Why was his light on?

Bea hesitated. Her dad wasn't due back till tomorrow. Had he come home early, or was that Mrs. Stickler tidying up? It seemed strange to be cleaning in the middle of the night. There were muffled scraping noises coming from inside, which sounded like drawers opening and closing.

Bea backed away and knocked into a side table. At once the noises stopped, and the study light switched off. Bea turned her flashlight off, too, and her heart thumped in the darkness. It couldn't be Mrs. Stickler in the study. If the housekeeper had heard a noise, she would have rushed out into the hallway immediately.

Bea stood frozen, her mind whirling. Maybe there was someone in the royal study who wasn't supposed to be there. Suddenly she remembered the flash of movement she'd seen outside the window the day before. If there was a burglar, she needed to get help right away.

But what if it was just her dad, who'd returned early? He'd want to know why she was out of bed, and he might ask what she'd done about Tiger.

The study light flicked back on, and the muffled sounds began again. Bea crept up to the door and knelt down beside the keyhole. There was a large black bag on the king's desk, and the crowns had disappeared.

At first Bea couldn't see who was inside. Then she caught a glimpse of a man in a gray jacket with a stubbly chin. It was the same man she'd seen walking across the palace garden earlier. Bea could hardly breathe. He must be stealing the royal treasures. She had to get help right away.

She scrambled to her feet, accidentally pressing on the door and pushing it open. The man swung around, his eyes narrowing. "Hey, what do you think you're doing?"

Bea took a step back, ready to run, but something moved at the top of the red velvet curtains. A furry orange tail swayed to and fro, and Tiger's little face peeked out from behind the curtain ruffles. The kitten wobbled as he padded along the curtain rod.

Bea stared in horror. If she ran to get help, she would be leaving Tiger in terrible danger.

The burglar grabbed his bag, knocking over a chair as he swung it across his shoulder. The chair fell to the floor with a clatter. Tiger meowed in surprise, and the burglar peered up at the little cat balanced on the curtain rod.

"Maybe you'll fetch me some money, too." The burglar snatched at the kitten.

"No!" Bea stepped forward. "Get away from him."

"Stay back or you'll be sorry!" the man snarled.

Tiger gave a squeaky kind of growl and tensed his body, ready to spring. His bottom wobbled, and for a second Bea was afraid he would fall. Then the little cat leapt from the curtain rod straight onto the burglar's head.

The man gave a roar, clutching at his hair.

"Well done, Tiger!" cried Bea. "Quickly, over here."

The kitten jumped onto the king's desk. The burglar made another grab for Tiger, but he lost his balance and staggered, catching hold of the curtains. There was a loud rip and the curtains fell off the rod, covering him completely.

"Princess Beatrice, are you all right? I heard you shouting." Mr. Wells rushed in, wearing slippers and pajamas. "What on earth is going on?"

The burglar struggled under the massive velvet curtains. His hands and elbows pushed out of the cloth in all directions.

"It's a burglar . . . ," Bea began breathlessly.

"What's going on?" Mrs. Stickler marched in, holding a frying pan as if it was a weapon.

"A burglar!" Mr. Wells scratched his head nervously. "It looks like Princess Beatrice caught him just in time."

"It was really Tiger that caught him," said Bea. "He was amazing!"

Tiger meowed proudly. Then he sat down on the king's desk and began cleaning his paws.

"Goodness! Is that the kitten you saved from the tree yesterday, Princess Beatrice?" asked Mr. Wells.

"Stand back, all of you!" Mrs. Stickler's eyes were fierce as she raised the frying pan in the air. She advanced on the burglar, who was still squirming under the heavy curtains. With her yellow satin dressing gown, her hair twisted into rollers, and streaks of face cream on her cheeks, she reminded Bea of a strange-looking warrior from ancient times.

"I'll fetch the grooms from the stables. They'll sort everything out." Mr. Wells hurried away, and Bea wasn't sure whether he was more scared of Mrs. Stickler or the burglar.

The grooms came quickly and took the burglar down to the police station.

Mrs. Stickler pulled the royal crowns out of the bag he'd left behind. Natasha and Alfie, who were woken by all the noise, came downstairs and stared wide-eyed at the messy study and the fallen curtains.

Bea explained what had happened. Tiger, who didn't seem the least bit tired, began pouncing on the wrinkled curtains.

"Nancy polished these crowns so nicely," grumbled Mrs. Stickler. "And now look at them! All smudged by dirty fingers."

"At least you caught the burglar before he got away," said Natasha.

"Sounds as if it was Tiger that did all the work," said Alfie. "He's like a super-cat! I wish I'd been here to see it all!"

Mrs. Stickler frowned at the kitten

and tutted, but she didn't disagree with Alfie.

Suddenly feeling very tired, Bea gathered Tiger into her arms and carried him upstairs. "You were so brave, Tiger!" she said as she put the kitten into his cat bed. "And you learned how to jump down from things at just the right moment. I'm so proud of you."

Tiger leapt out of his cat bed and settled down on Bea's pillow, purring against her cheek as they both fell into a deep sleep.

Chapter Nine

The Kitten and the King

King George returned the next morning and called everyone to a meeting in the palace parlor. Mrs. Stickler and Mr. Wells came in, followed by Mrs. Cherry and the grooms. Bea, Natasha, and Alfie sneaked in at the back to listen.

"I just wanted to thank those of you who stopped the burglar last night," began the king. "It must have taken great bravery and courage—"

"Tiger was the bravest one!" Alfie piped up. "He jumped off a curtain rod and landed on the burglar's head."

"Shh!" Bea nudged Alfie.

"What's that about a tiger?" King George looked confused.

"I believe Tiger is the name of the kitten, sire," explained Mr. Wells. "Princess Beatrice rescued the animal from a tree at the kite festival."

"That can't be right. I asked Beatrice to make sure the animal was gone before I returned." The king frowned. "Beatrice, where is this cat? Please fetch it immediately."

Bea went upstairs to get Tiger, who was fast asleep on her bed. She held the kitten tightly, pressing Tiger's warm fur to her cheek. There must be a way to change her dad's mind about letting Tiger stay. She had to at least try.

Hurrying into the parlor, she took a deep breath. "Dad, I want to tell you something about Tiger . . ."

The king stopped her. "Beatrice, Mrs. Brown has just arrived to tell us some news about your kitten." He pointed to Mrs. Brown, the kite festival organizer.

"Lots of people in town saw your Lost and Found posters, Princess Beatrice," Mrs. Brown explained. "But no one could figure out where your kitten had come from until we found a female cat with two more kittens under a bush near the beach. We think they must be from the same family, as they all have stripy orange fur just like this one."

"Why are they living by the beach?" asked Alfie.

"They must be strays," explained Mrs. Brown. "It was difficult finding homes for all of them, but we've managed it. I'm not sure we'd be able to find a place for your kitten, too."

"Oh!" Bea stroked the kitten's soft fur. "I'm glad the other kittens have new homes. I wish we could keep Tiger!"

The king cleared his throat. "I've always said there should be no animals here at Ruby Palace, and there are very good reasons for that rule. A palace is no place for a pet!"

"I think you're absolutely right, sire," Mrs. Stickler put in. "The creature would spread cat hairs everywhere!"

"But this little kitten is certainly quite the hero—capturing the burglar under a curtain like that," said Mr. Wells.

"Keeping a cat might scare rats away

from the stables, Your Majesty," said one of the grooms.

"A cat would scare the birds that peck at my strawberry plants, too," said Mrs. Cherry, the palace gardener.

Bea's heart lifted. She hadn't realized so many other people at the palace liked the idea of keeping a cat. She hugged Tiger hopefully.

"Yes, that's certainly true," King George said thoughtfully. "Perhaps there are a few good reasons for keeping this cat after all. But I can't have the creature running around when important guests come to visit."

"Maybe Tiger could sleep downstairs in the laundry room, out of everyone's way," suggested Natasha. "Then each day he could play in the stables and around the garden."

Bea looked at her sister gratefully. "I'm sure he'd really like that."

King George studied Tiger, who had curled up in Bea's arms. "Very well, then," he said slowly. "The kitten may stay, but he must keep out of the way and *never* run around in my royal study!"

Bea's heart leapt like a bouncy ball. "Thanks, Dad!"

"And make sure the cat doesn't get too pampered," the king added. "Animals shouldn't be spoiled with lots of treats and expensive toys."

Bea nodded meekly, but inside she felt so happy she thought she would burst!

Bea grabbed Fluff from Alfie's room the following morning. With Tiger sleeping in the laundry room, the little mouse would be safe in his box under her bed. She went to the schoolroom and began making a toy for the kitten when Alfie burst in.

"Mr. Wells wants you to come downstairs," he said breathlessly. "He needs to show us something important."

Alfie and Bea raced down the winding

stairs. Mr. Wells was waiting for them by the laundry room, his arms full of shopping bags. Tiger padded around Mr. Wells's feet, rubbing his head against the teacher's ankles.

"Your father asked me to pick up a few things the kitten might need from the shops," Mr. Wells explained. "I thought you could sort them out and put them in the laundry room."

"Wow, Tiger's got presents!" cried Alfie.

"Thanks, Mr. Wells," said Bea.

"You're welcome. It was all the king's idea." Mr. Wells smiled. "Now, remember: don't let Tiger sneak into the rest of the palace, or goodness knows what your father will say!" He handed them the shopping bags.

Alfie and Bea began unpacking

everything. They took out two green food bowls, a wooden scratching post, and two packets of cat food. Finally, Bea opened a box containing a beautiful cat bed lined with fluffy material and decorated with little paw prints. She smiled, thinking of how comfy Tiger would be sleeping on it.

"We can find out which of his new things Tiger likes best!" Alfie put the

bowls, the scratching post, and the fluffy cat bed in a row for the kitten to look at.

Tiger sniffed each thing carefully before moving on to the next. At last, the little kitten stopped beside the empty box that had contained the cat bed. Then he jumped inside and curled up with a happy meow.

"Tiger!" cried Alfie. "That's just a box."

Bea couldn't help giggling. She

gathered Tiger into her arms and pressed her cheek against the kitten's soft fur. The little cat would be happy and safe here at Ruby Palace.

This was just the beginning of her plan to help animals, and she was determined to look after as many as she could. That's what any animal-mad princess would do!

Thank you for reading this **Feiwel and Friends** book.

The Friends who made

ROYAL RESCUES

The Naughty Kitten

possible are:

Jean Feiwel, Publisher

Liz Szabla, Associate Publisher

Rich Deas, Senior Creative Director

Holly West, Senior Editor

Anna Roberto, Senior Editor

Kat Brzozowski, Senior Editor

Kim Waymer, Senior Production Manager

Cindy De La Cruz, Associate Designer

Avia Perez, Production Editor

Foyinsi Adegbonmire, Editorial Assistant

Rachel Diebel, Assistant Editor

Emily Settle, Associate Editor

Patrick Collins, Creative Art Director

Follow us on Facebook or visit us online at mackids.com

OUR BOOKS ARE FRIENDS FOR LIFE